KT-363-259

THE POOCHES

Heidi

Jake

Treacle

Samson

Riley

Molly

Gordon

Dither

Dash

Fiver

THE PLAN

Mayor Silverbottom's house

My house

School

Treacle's house

Molly's house

Princes Park

Gordon's house

DOGGY AEROBICS

RENFREWSHIRE COUNCIL	
244245521	
Bertrams	14/02/2018
	£5.99
REN	

Great Clarendon Street, Oxford OX2 6DP
Oxford University Press is a department of the University of Oxford.
It furthers the University's objective of excellence in research, scholarship,
and education by publishing worldwide. Oxford is a registered trade mark
of Oxford University Press in the UK and in certain other countries

Copyright © Clare Elsom 2018
Illustrations © Clare Elsom 2018

The moral rights of the author have been asserted

Database right Oxford University Press (maker)

First published 2018

All rights reserved. No part of this publication may be reproduced,
stored in a retrieval system, or transmitted, in any form or by any means,
without the prior permission in writing of Oxford University Press,
or as expressly permitted by law, or under terms agreed with the appropriate
reprographics rights organization. Enquiries concerning reproduction
outside the scope of the above should be sent to the Rights Department,
Oxford University Press, at the address above

You must not circulate this book in any other binding or cover
and you must impose this same condition on any acquirer

British Library Cataloguing in Publication Data

Data available

ISBN 978-0-19-275876-7

1 3 5 7 9 10 8 6 4 2

Printed in China

Paper used in the production of this book is a natural,
recyclable product made from wood grown in sustainable forests.
The manufacturing process conforms to the environmental
regulations of the country of origin.

HORACE
& Harriet

Every Dog Has Its Day

**WRITTEN AND ILLUSTRATED
BY THE SPLENDIFEROUS**

CLARE ELSOM

OXFORD
UNIVERSITY PRESS

Lord Commander Horatio Frederick
*illington Nincompoop Maximus
Pimpleberry the Third*

THE BIT WHERE I REMIND YOU WHAT'S GOING ON

This is Horace.

Or to give him his full name (you might want to take a deep breath here …): Lord Commander Horatio Frederick Wallington Nincompoop Maximus Pimpleberry the Third.

He lives in Princes Park.

If you walk around the park, you might see Horace doing some crazy things. Like the other day when I saw him trying to ride a bicycle he'd made out of old bits of junk.

It didn't go very well.

And the week before that he had an argument with the park swans. That didn't go very well either.

Oh, and did I mention that Horace is a statue? Who is 387 and a half years old? And that he's friends with a pigeon? Called Barry? Well, he's a statue who is 387 and a half years old, and he's friends with a pigeon called Barry.

And I'm Harriet. I live with my Fitness-Crazy Mum and Super-Clever Grandad in a house near Princes Park.

I first met Horace when he got really fed up with his pillar, and we searched the ENTIRE town trying to find somewhere else for him to live.

First he moved into Grandad's shed and decided to add cannons and a moat. Then he wanted me to help him invade horrible Mayor Silverbottom's mansion.

And it turns out that adventures involving ENTIRE-town-searching and sheds with cannons and near-invasions can actually make you really good friends.

Horace and Barry are Totally Brilliant Friends to have. They know every bit of

Princes Park, they make yummy sandwiches (although Horace eats most of them), and they stick up for me when Angela and her giggling gang call me names.

I've got some other Totally Brilliant Friends, who aren't statues or pigeons, and they're called Fraser and Megan. They live next door to each other and are always coming up with cool things for us to do.

Not statues or pigeons

Some people might find Horace embarrassing, but Fraser and Megan think he is hilarious.

Grandad and Horace are good friends too. They like to talk about their times in the navy. Mum doesn't *exactly* know about Horace. She did meet him, but just thought he was a normal statue, and Grandad said that's Probably For The Best. I'm not sure Mum could cope with Horace. Although, I'm not sure Horace could cope with Mum either. She'd probably take away his sandwiches and give him broccoli.

So, that's some stuff to know, and now I can tell you the whole story …

THE BIT WITH THE BEST EVER EXTRA IMPORTANT AND REALLY EXCITING HOLIDAY JOB

It was the start of the holidays and Fraser, Megan, and I had got The Best Ever Extra Important And Really Exciting Holiday Job ... *dog walking*!

Walking ACTUAL dogs.

I love dogs. I had already spent approximately 1,825 days persuading Mum to let me get a dog and it had *almost* paid off.

It usually went like this:

'Muuuuuuuum ...' (That's me saying that bit.)

'Yes, poppet?' (That's Mum talking now.)

'Canwegetadog Ireallywantadogand Iwouldloveitandlookafteritsowell pleasecanwecanwecanwe?!' (That's me again.)

'Well … maybe when you're A Bit Older.' (Mum again.)

I must have finally been A Bit Older (which is seven and a half, in case you're interested) because Mum was *almost* convinced! But she also said that having a dog was A Big Responsibility and I needed to show her I was ready.

Luckily, Mum really likes dogs too. As well as teaching yoga and kick-boxing and something called yoga-kick-boxing, she runs a Doggy Aerobics class, which

has got so popular that she does twenty sessions a week.

Lots of the dog owners from the class needed help with their dog walking, and *that's* where we came in. Mum suggested it to her customers, and there was so much interest that we had TEN dogs to walk every day in the summer holidays!

In the last week of school, Fraser and Megan and I spent our lunch breaks practising for our new job. We said 'SIT!' and 'FETCH!' in really loud voices, and picked up dog poo. (We actually picked up bouncy balls with our sandwich bags over our hands, which is less gross than actual dog poo, but it's good practice.)

Angela kept walking past us and coughing. The cough sounded suspiciously like the word 'losers', but we just ignored her while her gang giggled away.

   We decided Megan should be the leader, because she has a cat, which is the closest any of us have to a dog. I would be in charge of the schedule, and Fraser would be treasurer which meant he would look after all the money we earned. Which was going to be LOADS.

Fraser was saving up for some recording equipment. He wanted to make a remix of Horace playing his lute. Megan wanted new trainers. She's *so* fast at running and has just joined an athletics club. And I wanted the new *Dazzler the Dog* books.

A lute →

We also decided on a name.

'How about "The Dog Walking Demons"?' suggested Fraser, leaping up and posing like a superhero.

Megan wrinkled her nose. 'It doesn't sound very *friendly* ... How about "The Doggy Darlings"?'

Fraser made noises like he wanted to be sick.

'I think it needs to sound more grown-up,'

I said. 'How about: "We Are Three Very Serious Professional Dog Walking Experts Who Will Look After Your Dogs Really Well".'

The two of them considered it.

'It's not very snappy, is it?' said Fraser.

'Maybe get rid of some words?' suggested Megan.

We decided on Very Serious Professional Dog Walking Experts.

'We need a uniform!' I said. 'We need to look like a proper organisation.'

'Let's use our school t-shirts. We won't need them all summer!' Fraser suggested.

So, we drew our new logo on the back of our school t-shirts in permanent marker. (Our teacher was a bit cross about that.)

We also made badges to pin on the front. The whole name was a bit long to fit on

them, so my badge said: 'Very Serious',
Fraser's said: 'Professional Dog', and
Megan's said: 'Walking Expert'.

Fraser wasn't very happy with his, but I
thought they looked good, and Megan said
as long as we walked in a row it would all
be fine.

The only thing I was worried about was
that we planned to go to Princes Park
with the dogs. And you might remember

that Horace is just a *little* bit scared of dogs …

I decided I should prepare Horace about our new job, but the day Grandad and I went to the park to deliver the news, Horace was a little bit distracted.

By a dog.

Who was chasing him.

At first I thought he was having fun, but the terrified 'AAARRRGGGGHHHHHHH!' that Horace yelled as he fled past us made me think that he probably wasn't.

Other dogs thought it was fun though, and soon Horace was being chased around the park by a whole gang of them. He looked like he was winning a doggy marathon.

Horace eventually
made it back to the
pillar and lay down gasping
for breath.

'Dastardly hounds!' he panted. 'Can't eat
… a sandwich … without being tormented!'

I decided that it probably wasn't the
moment to tell Horace about our Best
Ever Extra Important And Really Exciting
Holiday Job.

But that was a WHOLE week before the holidays started, so perhaps he would have time to overcome his fear of dogs …

I hoped so.

THE BIT WHERE HORACE IS DEFINITELY STILL AFRAID OF DOGS

The first day of our new job was a *little* bit complicated.

'Shall we just collect them in alphabetical order?' asked Megan.

We were sitting in the kitchen with a map, and lists, and pens, and we were wearing our Very Serious Professional Dog Walking Experts uniforms.

We had ten dogs to pick up, which is not as easy as it sounds. And it doesn't even sound that easy.

'We can't …' I pointed out. 'Mr Poggety asked if Gordon could have the most possible exercise, so we need to collect him first.'

Gordon was a basset hound, who really needed to lose weight.

'OK, so, we'll get Gordon, then we could go down to get Riley and Samson, and then collect all the others on the way back to the park!' said Megan, pointing at the map.

'We can't,' said Fraser. 'That would mean taking Heidi to Mr Willis's house, and he has a cat ...'

Heidi was an Afghan hound, who belonged to Fraser's auntie and was scared of cats.

'So ... we'll get Gordon, *then* get Mr Willis's Dalmatian, *then* get Heidi, *then* get the others on the way back to the park?' asked Megan.

'We can't,' I said. 'That would mean we get Dash and Dither too late. They need to start their walk at exactly 10 o'clock on Mondays and Wednesdays.'

Dash and Dither were sausage dogs belonging to Mrs Zimman, who was

Dash

very strict about routines.

'Well … what do we do then?' said Megan, sounding worried.

'Hang on a minute,' said Fraser, staring at the map. He's good with puzzles.

'Got it,' he said finally. 'We get Gordon the basset hound, who needs the most exercise. Then we collect Molly—she belongs to the Spicklickets, so I say we do that REALLY fast so we don't have to talk to Angela. Then we get Dash and Dither, at 9.59 a.m., *then* we get Fiver the puppy and Jake the Dalmatian, who are both on Harrison Lane, *then* we cut through and get Heidi, avoiding the cat situation— which will take us right past the ice cream

Dither

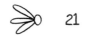

parlour—*then* we get Riley
the whippet and Samson the spaniel
from Ms Mendoza—they aren't meant to
have any treats, so we'll have to finish our
ice creams by then—and finally we get
Treacle the terrier, who's *ancient,* and won't
mind having the least walking time. Then
we drop them back in reverse order. Got it?
Right, let's go!'

'Slow down, Fraser!' said Megan, who was
tangled up in the leads of Gordon, Heidi,
Dash, and Dither.

'You try slowing down when you're being pulled along by four dogs!' said Fraser. *'Riley!* Heel!'

'I *am* being pulled along by four dogs!' said Megan.

We'd successfully collected all the dogs with only one teeny incident where Samson tried to chase a squirrel and Heidi tried to run away from it (turns out Heidi is afraid of cats *and* squirrels), and had almost reached the park.

Grandad was with us for the first day, to make sure everything went well.

'So, are we going to see Horace? Won't he be nervous of the dogs?' asked Megan, pulling Gordon away from eating some flowers.

'Well, these ones are *really* friendly,' I said, looking down. I had Molly and Fiver trotting along beside me. 'And anyway, Horace is made of stone—dogs can't hurt him!'

We got to the park. Grandad strolled off to a bench. The dogs all looked very excited and tried to go in different directions.

'I think you should hide in the bushes until I've prepared Horace ...' I said to Fraser and Megan nervously. I handed over Molly and Fiver's leads and marched over to Horace.

'Young Harriet!' Horace waved and clambered down. 'What a fine day to behold my young friend.'

'Hello, Horace!' I said. 'Your pillar is looking very nice today. Really, um ... stony.'

Horace beamed. 'Why thank you, Kind Child! I do my best. So, what intelligence do you have for me today? What shenanigans have unfolded of late?'

'Actually,' I said nervously, and glanced over
to where the others were hiding in the bushes.
I could see about six wagging tails poking
out. 'I do have some news. You know Fraser
and Megan …?'

'Of course! Your fine compatriots,' said
Horace.

'Yes, well, it's the summer holidays, and we
decided to get a job.'

'Employment, eh?' Horace chuckled. 'A noble challenge! And what do you …'

Suddenly I heard a shout from Megan. 'NO, Fiver! Sit! STAY!'

Before I could do anything, a tiny black and white blur shot out of the hedge and straight towards Horace.

Uh oh.

'AAAAAARRRGGGHHHHHH!!!'

Horace sprang backwards and tripped over. Fiver raced up and began licking his face.

I ran to pick up Fiver, and at that point

Jake, Samson, Riley, Heidi, Dash, Dither, Molly, and Treacle came bounding over too, pulling Fraser and Megan behind them. Even Gordon waddled as fast as he could.

'Sorry, Harri!' panted Megan. 'He just ran! I think he knew you had the treats in your pocket.'

'Hi, Horace!' shouted Fraser cheerily, over the barking of ten very excited dogs. 'How's the lute practice?'

'BLITHERING BARNACLES!' shrieked Horace, leaping back up on to his pillar. 'It's an ambuscade! Why on EARTH would you unleash these terrifying beasts on me? Back! Back, I say!'

The dogs sniffed excitedly around the
pillar and all at once cocked their legs.

'FOR GOODNESS' SAKE!' yelled
Horace. '*Barbarians!* Barry has spent all
morning polishing!'

'Oops, sorry, Horace,' said Megan.
'Maybe we'll take them on a run around
the park … Come on, Fraser!'

Fraser and Megan pulled the dogs away,

waving apologetically to Horace. I held onto Fiver.

'I'm *so* sorry, Horace,' I said. 'I wanted to explain before you saw them. I know you're not the biggest fan … but we're dog walkers now!'

Horace stared at me in horror.

'I thought you'd be pleased. It means I can come to the park to see you every single day!' I said encouragingly.

'With that slobbering, snarling beast in tow?!' said Horace, gesturing at Fiver.

'He's titchy, Horace, and really friendly!'
I said. 'Why don't you come and say hello?
I promise I'll hold on to him.'

'And take *my life* in my hands?!'
spluttered Horace. 'I think not. I will say
good day to you, young Harriet. I do not
wish to fraternize with these hideous
hounds. And … NOT AGAIN!'

Fiver lifted his leg against Horace's
pillar. I decided it was probably time to go.

I whispered an apology to Barry and
hurried to catch up with Fraser and
Megan.

Oh dear. That was NOT the start I had
hoped for.

THE BIT AFTER THE START I HADN'T HOPED FOR

A few days later, I went with Grandad to apologize to Horace again.

Horace peered through his telescope as we approached.

'Ah, my favourite naval companion. Good morning, sir!' he said to Grandad, pretending he didn't see me. 'What might you think of my latest pillar adornments?'

He gestured to some signs pinned to his pillar.

'Good morning, Horace!' said Grandad, and he saluted.

DOG
FREE
ZONE

DOGS NOT
WELCOME

HARRIET
NOT
WELCOME
IF SHE HAS
DOGS
WITH HER

'Morning, Horace,' I said nervously. I saluted as well and did it with both hands just to be extra polite.

Horace sniffed and raised one eyebrow. 'No four-legged pests with you this morning?' he asked.

'No … and I've come to apologize again, Horace. I really shouldn't have sprung the dogs on you like that. I've brought you some I'm Sorry Sandwiches. And pink lemonade! And banana chips for Barry!'

He peered at my offerings. 'Are they peanut butter sandwiches?' he asked eventually.

'Yes!' I said. 'With chocolate spread *and* marmalade!'

He seemed pleased.

'And I PROMISE never to let dogs jump on you again,' I said.

He looked at me and nodded. 'I do not desire to quarrel. We shall call it a truce, young Harriet!'

I breathed a huge sigh of relief, and Horace clambered down so we could all have sandwiches together.

'What's all this litter?' asked Grandad, nodding towards some balls of screwed-up paper.

Horace frowned. 'Well, after Harriet sought employment, I resolved to get a posting myself! The bother is these drivelling dalcops have no idea what a *fine* offer they have been made.' He waved at

the papers. 'Rejections, the lot of them!'
He chomped his sandwiches crossly.
I unscrewed one of the bits of paper:

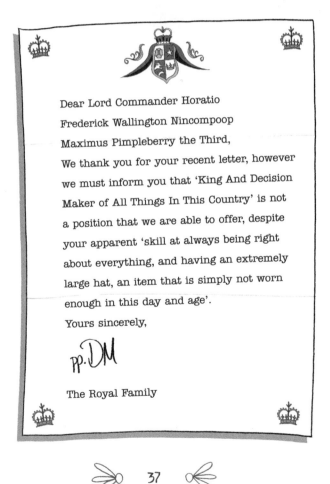

Dear Lord Commander Horatio
Frederick Wallington Nincompoop
Maximus Pimpleberry the Third,
We thank you for your recent letter, however
we must inform you that 'King And Decision
Maker of All Things In This Country' is not
a position that we are able to offer, despite
your apparent 'skill at always being right
about everything, and having an extremely
large hat, an item that is simply not worn
enough in this day and age'.
Yours sincerely,

pp. DM

The Royal Family

I gulped and looked at another one:

Dear Mr the Third,

We appreciate your recent correspondence, but regret to inform you that 'Medal Model' is not a vacancy we have available, although we note with interest that you have 'the finest medals ever seen on any statue, especially compared to that idiot Cuthbert Silverbottom'.

We also want to clarify that we sell model aeroplanes.

Best wishes,

Sylvia Fisher

Sylvia Fisher

Director of Model Mania

I cringed and looked at a third one:

Dear Horatio,

While we are aware of the Pimpleberry family's nautical legacy, and admire your ambition regarding your desire to be 'Head of the Navy', we suggest you begin with some military experience at a significantly lower level.

We have also had an incident brought to our attention involving a pedalo in Princes Park, and suggest that you may wish to brush up on your seafaring skills before applying for any maritime positions.

I enclose a pamphlet listing junior sailing groups in your area.

Regards,

Admiral Hollingsworth

Admiral Hollingsworth
First Sea Lord and Chief of Naval Staff

I blinked and put them down.

'Are you … aiming a *teeny* bit too high, Horace?' I suggested.

'TOO HIGH?!' spluttered Horace, looking outraged. 'Those incompetent swines should be grateful I deigned to offer my expertise!'

I didn't want Horace to be cross with me again, so I decided to stay quiet.

'Come on, Harri, time to go,' said Grandad, gathering up the sandwich wrappers. 'Best forget about these, Horace,' he said gently, throwing the letters in the recycling bin.

'Something is bound to come up!' I said, giving his stony hand a squeeze.

I racked my brains as
we walked away. Surely
there must be a job
perfect for Horace?

HARRIET
NOT
WELCOME
IF SHE HAS
DOGS
WITH HER

THE BIT WITH THE PERFECT JOB FOR HORACE

The next morning we collected Gordon (who tried to eat everything), Molly (who jumped in a muddy puddle), Dash and Dither (who ran around my legs until I tripped up), Fiver (who chewed on Fraser's shoe), Jake

(who
needed to wee
17 times), and Heidi (who
hid behind a tree when she
saw a ladybird), and were finally
on our way to Ms Mendoza's house.

'Poor Horace!' said Megan. 'I
can't believe the navy wouldn't
give him a job.'

'Well, would you
trust Horace to
sail a ship?' asked
Fraser.

'I think he'd almost
definitely sink it … *No,
Jake!* Not on the flowers!'
Ms Mendoza was
on the phone when we
arrived and looked a bit
frazzled. She's the editor of
a newspaper called *The Buzz*,
and is always running around
looking busy.

'I just don't know WHAT
to do,' she was saying.

'That's the third member of staff to leave within the month! I'm simply *desperate*.'

My ears pricked up.

'Who is going to cover the awards ceremony tomorrow evening?' she wailed. 'We need someone *immediately*!'

She rang off and turned to us with a sigh.

'Is everything OK, Ms Mendoza?' I asked politely while I tried to clip leads onto Samson and Riley, who were bouncing up and down like yo-yos.

'Hmm? No, not really, Harriet, I'm having an absolute nightmare getting enough staff for the paper. At my wits' end! I don't suppose you could turn your hand to journalism as well as dog walking, could you?' she laughed.

'Journalism? Is that like writing?' Megan asked from the doorway.

'Ah, I'm pretty good at writing!' said Fraser. 'I got a B for my last English project, didn't I, Megan? I …'

'What would someone have to do to get the job Ms Mendoza?' I asked excitedly, elbowing Fraser.

'At this stage, just be available and willing to work, pronto!' she said, and showed us an advert asking for writers in the last edition of *The Buzz*. 'I must make a few more calls now. See you soon!'

We skipped off with the dogs.

'Horace would be *totally* perfect for working on the paper!' I burst out, as soon as we were outside. 'He's brilliant with words! OK, he uses some pretty weird

ones … but he'd be great!'

'Horace will want to find it himself,' Megan pointed out, 'so how do we make him see the advert?'

Luckily I knew just the person—or to be precise, pigeon—to handle this.

We got to Princes Park and hid behind the bandstand. I didn't think Horace could handle a doggy encounter today.

'We need to attract Barry's attention!' I said. 'Can you do a pigeon noise, Fraser?'

Fraser shrugged. 'TWIT TWOO!' he

yelled. Gordon and Heidi started howling.

'That's an owl!' said Megan.

'Well, it's basically the same! You try!'
said Fraser.

'C-caw?' tried Megan.

'That was like a diseased parrot!' said
Fraser.

I sighed. But then I saw Barry flap over
to us, probably wondering what these
weird birds were doing in his park.

'Barry!' I said excitedly, as he landed on

my shoulder. 'Will you
do us a favour? We
think we have found
JUST the job for
Horace ...'

The next morning I woke up to a familiar tapping sound.

Tap. Tap-tap-tap. Taptaptaptap.

I leapt out of bed to open the window, and Barry flapped in with a rolled-up note:

Harriet,

No doubt you will hear that I have been engaged as Lead Correspondent on **The Buzz**! I spotted a plea for the 'finest writers in the land' in Barry's newspaper. Most fortuitous! Tough competition, of course, but I merely explained who I was and they begged me to start post-haste. I dare say the whole town is talking about it!

Yours importantly,

Horatio

I grinned, and gave Barry a feathery high five.

Fraser and Megan arrived, and I showed them the note. 'Mega!' said Fraser. 'Nice work, Barry!'

When we got to Mr Willis's house, Jake the Dalmatian was looking very gloomy and wearing a big plastic cone.

'What's wrong with his neck?' asked Megan.

'He hurt his ear, poor thing,' said Mr Willis. 'Has to keep the collar on so he doesn't scratch it. That reminds me—

could you drop into the vet's and pick up Jake's medicine? I can pay a bit extra for the detour.'

Fraser made a note. We were always being asked to do extra things for the owners, but we didn't mind. Our Very Serious Professional Dog Walking Experts' money jar was getting fuller by the day!

'Poor Jake!' said Megan, giving him a scratch. 'We'll make sure the other dogs are especially nice to you.'

'I wouldn't count on Molly. She does belong to Angela ...' muttered Fraser, glancing at the little Maltese terrier.

Jake didn't walk very fast with his cone on, so we paired him up with Treacle, who was REALLY old, Fiver, who had tiny

legs, and Gordon, who was still a bit slow.

At Princes Park, Horace's pillar was looking a little, um, different.

'Does he have an *office*?!' asked Megan.

Then Barry flew over and landed on my shoulder, looking very sulky. 'Er, I'll go and investigate,' I said, bounding over to Horace.

'Hi, Horace! What's wrong with Barry?' I asked.

'Alas, he is not in the best disposition!' said Horace. 'I required a quill … and he wasn't too forthcoming in giving me one of his feathers.'

Barry glared at him.

'Well, it's *brilliant* news about *The Buzz*!' I said.

Horace puffed out his chest proudly. 'It

certainly is. They are MOST delighted to have me on board. My first job begins this very eve, covering the *Stars of Stokendale* awards!' He gestured to his pillar. 'Behold all this equipment! I have a lapped top with why five, no less!'

'Er, do you mean a laptop with Wi-Fi?' I asked Horace. 'Fraser could help. He's brilliant with computers!'

'No time, the article will be published on the morrow. I shall be working through the night to submit in a timely fashion! I shall not disturb young Fraser— Barry and I can get to grips with these devices!' said Horace, opening the laptop upside down.

I felt a bit unsure about that. He fiddled with a Very Expensive-Looking camera and jumped as the flash went off.

'Zarbles! That near blinded me! The only bother is,' Horace went on, frowning, 'the event is hosted by that *fool* of a mayor ...'

'Mayor Silverbottom?' I asked, horrified. Mayor Silverbottom was a descendant of Horace's arch-enemy, Cuthbert, and it was NOT a good idea to have them in the same room together.

'Yes,' said Horace. 'But ne'er worry, fair Harriet! I plan to spend as little time as possible near that buffoon. It is due to be rather a glamorous affair, you know.

Annual highlight of the calendar! I shall polish my medals. Barry is planning to wear a top hat!'

I felt a bit unsure about that, too.

'Well, I must hurry you along, Harri. There are preparations to be done!' He picked up a new phone and jabbed at a recording app. 'TESTING. ONE, TWO, THREE!' he bellowed into it.

Barry jumped.

I couldn't help but feel a bit nervous …

THE BIT WHERE I WAS RIGHT TO FEEL A BIT NERVOUS

'*Behold!*' Horace announced as he strolled into the garden the following morning, waving a newspaper excitedly.

'Horace!' Grandad greeted him with a slap on the back, and then winced. You sometimes forget Horace is made of stone. 'First article is out, eh?'

'Forsooth! *Centre spread,*' said Horace, beaming. 'I have been up all night submitting my story. We haven't slept, have we, Barry?'

'Read it out, Grandad!' I said, excited.

Grandad flicked through the paper, smiling.
Then he stopped smiling. Then he looked
a bit confused. Then he spat out his tea.

'What?' I said. I looked over Grandad's shoulder at the paper.

'Is it … *just* pictures of you and Barry, Horace?' I asked, looking up.

'Nay, there are plentiful words!' said Horace. '*Perchance* not as plentiful as requested, but this "typing" tomfoolery is a tricky business. Barry can only peck one letter at a time.'

atio Frederick Wallington Pimpleberry the Third Stars of Stokendale

The most handsome attendee

The best speech of the evening

Grandad turned the page and read out: '*We asked a few attendees what they liked best about Stokendale. Naturally, they said that it was me!*'

Grandad and I stared at Horace.

'I *presume* the people think that,' said Horace. 'I failed to operate the recording device, whereupon I resolved to be inventive!'

'You made things up?!' Grandad asked, looking worried.

'Not all of it,' said Horace. 'Keep reading!'

Grandad continued, '*The evening was lowered in tone by the constant appearance of the loathly Mayor Silverbottom and his giant nose. The food was lacking in finesse, with no provision of sandwiches whatsoever, and people*'

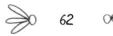

were attired in the usual sub-standard dress of
the modern times.'

Oh dear.

Grandad looked a bit pale.

'Did you, um, include who won the
awards?' I asked hopefully.

'Not important!' Horace scoffed.

Luckily we were saved from saying
anything else by a sudden ringing.

Horace rummaged in his pockets and
pulled out his phone. 'Lord Commander
Horatio Fr ...' he began in his booming
voice, but fell silent as an even louder
squawking at the end of the phone
drowned him out.

'How did this even get printed?'
whispered Grandad to me. 'Did no one
check it?'

'I think Horace just uploads the article!'
I whispered back.

Horace threw his phone at the shed,
looking very cross.

'I have been
DEMOTED.
Demoted! The
indignity!' he

spluttered. 'Ms Mendoza instructed me to write an *apology*, for failing to report on key events. And for the remark about Silverbottom's nose!'

'Well, I know he's not very nice, but you were a bit rude ...' I started.

'I fail to see the problem. It's *HUMONGOUS*!' said Horace, outraged.

'I'm surprised you've not been fired, Horace!' said Grandad, with a twinkle in his eye. Grandad quite liked a bit of drama.

'Nay, she does not wish to dispose of my extensive talents,' sighed Horace. 'They want me to write an advice column instead! I am forbidden to talk to people, apparently.'

Barry needed a rest, so we left Horace

writing in the shed, grumbling to himself, and went out on Very Serious Professional Dog Walking Experts duty.

Fraser had to stop and bend over because he was laughing so hard when I told him the bit about Mayor Silverbottom and Horace calling his nose humongous.

'Oh dear,' said Megan. 'I can't believe Ms Mendoza let him stay! What's he going to write for his advice column?!'

That's *exactly* what I was worried about.

We picked up Gordon and went over to the Spicklickets' house to get Molly.

'It's your turn today, Harri,' said Megan. We had been taking it in turns to go to

the Spicklickets' front door. I groaned
and knocked.

Angela answered it, glaring at me. 'My
mum was at the awards ceremony last
night, and your weird friend Horace was
VERY rude to her. He said that her dress
looked like a lampshade.'

I heard Fraser snort behind me.

'My mum is friends with Mayor Silverbottom, you know, *and* Ms Mendoza,' Angela continued. 'She can get Horace FIRED. Oh, and you need to give Molly a bath before you bring her back. She rolled in the compost heap this morning, and *I'm* not cleaning her up.'

Then she flounced off into her house and slammed the door. I bent down to give poor Molly a pat. She smelled of rotten cabbages.

'Well, let's look on the bright side,' said Fraser, holding his nose. 'I don't think it will be Angela's mum who gets Horace fired. I'm pretty sure he'll do that all on his own.'

'How on earth is that a bright side?' I asked.

THE BIT WHERE THE PROBLEMS CONTINUE

'*Help from Horace,*' I read out. '*…Because you certainly need it!*'

I looked up from *The Buzz*, where I was reading Horace's new column.

'Snappy title, eh?' said Horace, looking proud.

'Um …' I said. I thought it was a bit rude actually, but this *was* Horace we were talking about. At least he hadn't insulted anyone's nose yet.

'*How to Make a Ruff,*' I continued. I looked up at Horace. 'What's a ruff?'

'Read on, my curious companion, read on!'

I looked at the article. There were a lot of complicated pictures showing you how to make a weird lace collar thing for your neck.

'Now, you are no doubt desperate to dash off and create your own ...' said Horace.

'Oh, um ... *absolutely.*'

HELP FROM HORACE
...Because you certainly need it!
HOW TO MAKE A RUFF:

HOW TO ARRANGE YOUR MEDALS:
HOW TO DARN YOUR BREECHES:
TIP:

(I decided it would be OK to tell a fib here.)

'But NEVER fear, young Harriet. I have created one for you!'

I stared, a bit gobsmacked, as Horace presented me with one of the weird lace collar things. Was I meant to WEAR that?

'Er, thanks, Horace! But … I don't think it will go with my outfit.' I looked down at my jeans and t-shirt hopefully.

'Nonsense. It can be worn with everything!' said Horace cheerily.

Oh dear.

I double-crossed my fingers that no one from my school would walk past and tied the ruff around my neck.

'Marvellous! Significant improvement.

Barry liked his too. Come out, Barry! Don't be shy.'

I looked at the rest of the article. '*How to arrange your medals ... How to darn your breeches ...*' I continued. 'What's a darn? Hang on ... *How to heat your residence with horse manure ...*' I stared at Horace. 'Horse poo? Who is going to use horse poo in their houses?'

I wasn't sure this would be *exactly* the advice that Ms Mendoza wanted for her paper.

Horace was waiting with his

eyebrows raised.

'So, it all sounds *great*,' I began (that might have been a fib again), 'but is it … a little bit … old-fashioned?' I tried.

'Old-fash—?' Horace started, but then his mobile phone rang.

'Horatio speaking!' he boomed into the phone.

I heard the angry squawking at the other end again, confirming that it was not *exactly* the advice that Ms Mendoza wanted for her paper.

'FIRED?' he roared into the phone. 'Now, listen here—I have not been dismissed from a post since 1658, and that was for invading the wrong country!' he said. He strode off with the phone, and a concerned Barry flew after him.

Poor Horace. He might be a bit, um, Horace-y, but he didn't mean any harm, really.

Suddenly I heard an explosion of laughter.

I turned around to see Fraser and

Megan, and Fraser was pointing at me.

'Wha … hahaha … wha … HAHA! What is *THAT*?'

I scowled at him. 'It's a present from Horace. It's called a *ruff* actually.'

'You look like Jake!' Fraser managed to blurt out, before collapsing again.

Even Megan giggled.

'Horace has been fired from *The Buzz*,' I said to Megan, ignoring Fraser because he was Being Very Immature, and told her all about the latest article. 'He'll be really upset. We have to find a way to cheer him up!'

Suddenly Fraser stopped laughing and stared at a man walking towards us.

The man nodded at me as he walked past.

Fraser stared with his mouth open.

'Was he wearing …?' he asked.

'*Yes,*' Megan and I replied together.

'Fiver, Molly, stop messing around!' said Fraser, as the two little dogs played tug of war with Fraser's shoelaces.

We had collected Gordon, Molly, Dash, Dither, Fiver, Jake, Heidi, Samson, and Riley, and arrived to get Treacle from Mr Ramad's house.

Mr Ramad's twin daughters, who were Much Older And Too Cool To Talk To Us, were sunbathing in the front garden

and playing on their phones.

'I'm, like, *totally* going to be making one,' said Samira.

'Like, *totally*,' agreed Safia. 'Mum has some lace somewhere. I'll measure your neck!'

Fraser, Megan, and I looked at each other in amazement.

That afternoon while we
were walking the dogs, we saw *fifteen*
people wearing ruffs. And a few more with
medals and hats that looked quite a lot like
Horace's.

'I don't believe this,' I said, staring at a
couple who had matching spotty ruffs.

'Put yours back on, Harri!' said Megan.

'No! It makes me look like a clown!' I
said.

'At least we know a way to cheer Horace
up!' said Fraser. 'You know, I think I might
make one when I get home.'

THE BIT WHERE THE PROBLEMS CONTINUE TO CONTINUE

The next day I woke up to more tapping at my window. Barry was still wearing his ruff.

Harriet,

You will be delighted to hear that **The Buzz** realized the error of their ways and reappointed me! The 'online version' of my article has 'gone viral'. While this may sound like the plague, it actually means I am even more popular than we all thought.

More soon!

Horatio (of 'Help from Horace' fame)

Brilliant! Things were looking up!

I could hear the phone ringing and dashed to get it. 'Hello?'

'Harri? It's Megan,' she said, sounding excited. 'Horace's article has been shared online 879,954 times!! And there are SO many ruff selfies!'

'879,962!' I heard Fraser shout from the background.

'I know!' I said. 'I just got a note from Barry. Horace has been rehired!'

'879, 974 times!' Fraser shouted. 'He's OFFICIALLY more popular than the cat with the saucepan video!'

'OK, Fraser …' said Megan. 'Right, better go. My mum will drop us off with you in half an hour.'

Megan rang off, to the sounds of '*879,992 …!*'

We collected Gordon, then Molly, then Dash and Dither at exactly 9.59 a.m. because it was a Wednesday, and then went to collect Fiver from the Lochfords.

Mr Lochford answered the door, but I could hardly see him behind the giant box he was holding.

'Harriet!' he greeted me. 'Thanks *so* much for all this dog walking. Bit manic here. We move at the weekend! Off to sunnier climates in Brazil!'

'That's OK,' I said, then whispered so the other dogs didn't hear. 'Fiver is one of my favourites!'

'The little angel is rather under our feet today,' said Mrs Lochford, coming to the door with Fiver. 'We have *so* much packing

to do. Toodle-oo!' she trilled.

We collected the other dogs and arrived at Princes Park.

'Horace is never going to get over his fear if we keep avoiding him when we're with the dogs,' grumbled Fraser. 'And we want to show him our ruffs! Why don't you take Fiver over to see how he handles it? He's no bigger than Barry!'

'But it was Fiver who jumped on him,' I said uncertainly.

'That took him by surprise,' Megan said. 'Maybe if you go slowly, he'll see you coming and feel less nervous?'

'I'll give it a go,' I agreed. I approached Horace's pillar with Fiver, going nice and slowly.

'*... Shakespeare, a rather talented new*

author …' Horace was saying, while
Barry pecked at the laptop. 'Come, Barry,
that's not how you spell Shakespeare! Oh,
greetings, Harri!'

'Hello, Horace!' I waved. 'I'm *so* happy you
got your job back!'

Horace beamed. '*Help From Horace* lives
on!' he said, looking smug. 'Though, Ms
Mendoza is rather tiresome. Terribly strict.
Only an afternoon to get the next column
finished, and if I write anything out of place
she'll be rid of me again!'

'Well, you *have* to do what they tell you
this time, Horace,' I warned.

I suddenly noticed that Horace had
climbed down from his pillar and wasn't
making any fuss about Fiver!

'Horace!' I said proudly. 'You're facing

your doggy fear! You don't seem at all bothered by Fiver.'

Horace looked confused. 'What's that? There is no hound here, young Harriet!'

'What?' I swung around … to see an empty collar at the end of the lead.

Oh. My. Goodness.

'Fiver?' I called, feeling a bit panicky in my tummy. 'FIVER!'

I dashed over to Fraser and Megan. 'Have you seen Fiver?' I asked them desperately.

'What? No, he was with you!' said Megan.

'You're not meant to let him off the lead, Harri. He's too young!' said Fraser.

'*I didn't,*' I wailed. 'He must have slipped out of his collar. What am I going to do? FIVER!'

Barry flapped over to me looking curious.

'Barry,' I said

desperately, 'Please go and fetch Grandad. It's an emergency!'

Barry flew off immediately.

Grandad arrived at the park only five minutes later, puffing and panting. I told him what had happened, and he went straight over to Horace.

'Commander,' Grandad said to him. 'We have an emergency situation and need your assistance. We must deploy a search of the area, immediately.'

'You wish me to help track a pup?' Horace stared at the other dogs, who were edging closer to

his pillar. He shook his head. 'Nay, Harriet
… I must get the column finished. The
people need *Help from Horace*!'

Horace turned away.

I swallowed. I felt disappointed. *I* needed
help from Horace.

'It's OK, Horace,' I said to him. 'I know
you don't want anything to do with the
dogs. You should definitely focus on
getting your column written.'

I waited. (I was doing That Thing Where You Say One Thing And Hope Another Thing Will Happen.)

But Horace just stayed where he was, tapping at the laptop with Barry.

Barry looked apologetic.

Grandad turned to us with a sigh. 'OK. Come on, team, it's just us. Let's start hunting!'

We searched Princes Park, going around to *every* single corner and looking under

every single bush. We searched our whole dog-walking route. We searched near Mum's Doggy Aerobics class. We even searched the pet shop.

'He might have smelled the dog food,' Fraser pointed out.

But we couldn't find little Fiver anywhere.

Eventually we had to take the other dogs back home.

I handed over my 'Very Serious' badge

to Megan. I didn't deserve it.

Megan gave me a hug.

'Don't worry, Harri,' said Fraser. 'We'll find Fiver tomorrow, I know it! I'm going to research Dog Detection when I get home!'

Grandad and I went back to Mr and Mrs Lochford's house.

Grandad explained what had happened: how Fiver had slipped out of his collar and how we'd searched Absolutely Everywhere and we were Really Very Terribly Sorry and we would Do Everything We Possibly Could to help find their puppy.

Mrs Lochford burst into tears.

So did I.

Mr Lochford
looked REALLY
PROPER
cross, like
Mum
looked
when she
discovered
cannons on her
shed.

'We're
moving house
in two days,
to a *different
country*!' he
exploded.

'We'll never find Fiver in time!'

We walked back home, and Grandad gave me a hug. 'It was an accident, Harri. It wasn't your fault,' he said gently. He made me Cheer-Up Chocolate Milkshake, but I couldn't drink it, even though it had extra cream *and* sprinkles on top.

'Try not to worry,' Grandad said. 'We've reported the pup as missing, and we've searched all we can today. I'm *sure* Fiver will turn up. He's a clever little fellow.'

I know Grandad was trying to make me feel better, but I had never felt so Completely And Absolutely Terrible in my whole life.

THE BIT WHERE THE PROBLEMS STOP CONTINUING

'How about we make some posters?' suggested Fraser. 'They could say FREE ICE CREAM and have a picture of Fiver on them.'

Megan and I stared at him.

'Why would they say FREE ICE CREAM?' Megan asked.

'Because people are more interested in free ice creams than missing dogs!' Fraser rolled his eyes, like it was obvious.

'I don't think we have time. We have to

find Fiver by tonight!' I wailed.

We were in the kitchen having a Very Serious Professional Dog Walking Experts meeting. Fiver had been missing for 23 hours and 14 minutes, and we were running out of time before the Lochfords left for Brazil the next day.

We all jumped when there was a loud rapping at the window. It was Horace.

Grandad opened the door.

'Good morning, compatriots!' Horace

announced cheerfully, strolling in with
Barry.

'Morning, Horace,' I mumbled. I still felt
cross with him for not helping us yesterday.

'Hark! The new *Help from Horace* is out
today,' he said, waving a copy of *The Buzz*.

'I'm not really in the mood, Horace,'
I said. 'We need to find
Fiver, *remember*?'

Horace continued
to flick through the
newspaper. 'Ready? I
shall read it out …'

I felt REALLY
cross then. I
was *always* helping
Horace, and when

I needed *his* help, he only cared about his article!

I started to stomp upstairs with my I'm Actually Very Cross With You face on.

'Um, Harri,' said Megan slowly, 'you might want to see this.'

I paused mid-stomp. Megan held up the newspaper.

HELP FROM HORACE

EMERGENCY: HELP FIND MISSING HOUND

I stared at the article.

'Horace,' I said. 'But, but … I thought you weren't helping. I thought you didn't care!'

'I resolved to use my extreme popularity for a good cause,' said Horace. 'Never leave a soldier behind! Even if that soldier has an uncommon fondness for canines.' He shuddered.

'*Strange-looking mutt with big ears and goggly eyes,*' Fraser read from the article. 'Well, it does the job!'

'But you're going to be in trouble again, Horace!' I suddenly realized. 'Ms Mendoza will be *so* cross you didn't write your advice column!'

As if by magic, Horace's phone rang.

'*Help from Horace,*' he answered.

We could hear snippets of Ms Mendoza's shouts as Horace held the phone away from his ear. '*THIS WAS YOUR FINAL WARNING. READERS WILL THINK THE PAPER IS A JOKE! THIS TIME, YOU'RE FIRED, HORATIO!*'

Horace put the phone back in his pocket. 'She was … a little vexed,' he said.

'Horace, I'm so sorry!' I said. 'It's all my fault!'

'Do not feel troubled, Harriet,' Horace said. 'Henceforth, I leave *The Buzz* behind me. Grander ventures are ahead!' He winked

  100

at Fraser, who winked back at Horace.

'What are you two up to?' Megan asked curiously.

'Nothing!' they both said, in a way you knew there was *Definitely* Something.

'So, what happens now?' I asked, pointing at the article. 'Do we just sit around waiting for the phone to ring ag—?'

The phone rang again.

'*Help from Horace!*' answered Horace.

Horace nodded and made 'mm-hmm' noises into the phone until I was nearly bursting with suspense. He hung up and turned to us.

'Fiver …' Horace began.

Grandad crossed his fingers.

Megan crossed her legs.

I crossed my arms.

Fraser crossed his eyes and stuck his tongue out.

'… has been located!' said Horace, proudly. 'We can go and retrieve him forthwith!'

'Woohoo!' I yelled.

'Mega!' shouted Fraser.

'*Excellent!*' laughed Megan.

'Thank goodness,' muttered Grandad.

'To Princes Park!'

cried Horace, and he charged off, leading the way.

✿ ✿ ✿

We arrived panting at Horace's pillar.

Sure enough, there was Fiver! He was looking happy as anything in the arms of a friendly looking woman.

'You must be Horace!' she said. 'I'm Martha. I saw your article this morning, which made me check my shed. Sure enough, there was little Fiver, fast asleep curled up on a sack!'

'A *thousand* thanks to you, kind maiden,' said Horace, saluting.

Fraser, Megan, and I saluted too.

'Hey, that's the little dog from the paper this morning!' said a man, stopping to peer at Fiver.

'Goodness, there he is!' said a woman,

 103

overhearing. 'Dorothy, come and see!'

'*And there's Horace!*' cried another woman. 'I *love* your articles!'

Before we knew it a crowd had gathered, all peering at Fiver and trying to talk to Horace.

Horace was in his element. 'All in a day's work, no bother, no bother,' he said to the crowd, beaming. 'Why, of course I can sign your ruff!' he said to a couple who had run up to him.

Fiver gave a happy little bark.

'Here you are!' laughed Martha, and she held out Fiver to Horace.

Fraser, Megan, and I all froze.

'Oh no,' whispered Megan.

There was a pause, and Horace looked a bit terrified.

But as the crowd all waited expectantly,

Horace slowly reached out and took the little dog.

Fiver nuzzled into Horace and gave him a lick. I heard Horace let out a small squeak, but he managed to stay where he was.

The crowd all cheered.

'Horace, smile!' called Megan, and she clicked a photo with Horace's camera.

I felt SO relieved and happy that I did a little dance around Horace's pillar. Barry and Fraser and Megan joined in.

Grandad said his knees were A Bit Old For That, but he was VERY relieved.

Horace declared that our dancing looked extremely undignified but he was delighted he could be of service and 'could we *please* go and be rid of this pup now?!'

The Lochfords looked surprised to see so many people on their doorstep. As well as me, Horace, Fraser, Megan, and Grandad, Martha and several other people from the park had come along to

see the grand reunion.

'FIVER!' Mr Lochford exclaimed, as Horace stepped forward.

'My baby!' Mrs Lochford shrieked. She scooped up Fiver, burst into tears again, and gave Horace a kiss on the cheek.

Horace went a bit pink, but looked very pleased. 'You're most welcome, madam,'

he said. He even managed to give Fiver another pat before we left.

'Well done, Horace!' I whispered, and we grinned at each other.

🐾🐾🐾

After lunch, Fraser and Megan helped me make an 'I'm Sorry Again That I Lost Your Dog But I'm So Relieved He Was Found And I Hope You All Have Fun In Brazil' card for the Lochfords, and we had chocolate milkshakes with extra cream and sprinkles, even though I didn't need cheering up any more.

'So, with Fiver off to Brazil, that must mean you have a spot free in your group?' Mum asked, when she came home from teaching Doggy Aerobics.

'That's right!' I said. 'Is there another dog that needs walking?'

'Well, I think there might be,' said Mum, smiling. 'How about we take a trip to the doggy rescue centre this afternoon? Finally get you a dog of your own?'

I looked up, startled.

'But I lost Fiver!' I blurted out. 'I didn't think I'd EVER be allowed a dog after that! Or at least until I was *Really* Quite A Bit Older!'

'What happened with Fiver was an accident, poppet,' Mum said, sitting down and holding my hand. 'You learned a lesson and handled it brilliantly. I'm very proud. You have *definitely* understood the responsibility that comes with having a dog.'

Megan squealed in excitement and handed me back my 'Very Serious' badge.

'Very Serious Professional Dog Walking Experts forever!' cried Fraser, and we did our special three-way handshake.

I couldn't believe it. I was going to get my own dog! This was the Best Day EVER!

THE BIT WHERE I WRAP EVERYTHING UP

Let me introduce you to *Tiger*!!

He ran up to me the second we got to the rescue centre. Mum said it was love at first lick. He's a chihuahua, which means he is really small and Absolutely, Completely Brilliant. Since Horace helped with Fiver, he's been a bit better around dogs and even took Tiger for a walk with me the other day! We offered him a special position as a Very Serious Professional Dog Walking Expert, but he replied, 'I would rather cut Cuthbert's toenails.' So, I'm not sure he *completely* loves dogs yet.

Loads of people heard about Horace finding Fiver, because the photograph that Megan took was published in a big newspaper. We offered it to *The Buzz* first, but Ms Mendoza said she'd 'Had Quite

△ THE INQUIRER △

EVERY DOG HAS ITS DAY

PHOTO BY MEGAN ROBERTS

Enough Of Horace For A Lifetime Thank You Very Much'.

The 'Definitely Something' that Horace and Fraser were up to turned out to be that they have started a blog! *Help from Horace* was so popular that Horace kept writing it, and now Fraser puts it online. He can type much faster than Barry. Horace is back to writing with a feather quill, though, which doesn't make Barry very happy.

Horace's advice is still a bit, well, Horace-y, but people seem to like it.

The Very Serious Professional Dog Walking Experts became even *more* popular when people heard how well we dealt with the Fiver situation. I suggested we quit school and be dog walkers forever, but Mum wasn't keen on that idea, so we have decided to carry on just at weekends.

With all the money we earned over the summer, Fraser, Megan, and I had enough for our new recording equipment and trainers and *Dazzler the Dog* books ... but we actually decided to use our wages for something else.

We gave a shiny wrapped present to Horace, and he tore it open.

'A camera!' he exclaimed.

'It's to say thank you for helping us out,' I explained. 'To replace the one that belonged to *The Buzz*.'

Horace was delighted. 'A splendiferous gift! I shall take photos for my blog!'

'And you can keep a record of your adventures,' said Megan.

'And disasters,' muttered Fraser, grinning.

There did always seem to be a lot of both when Horace was around.

Grandad took the first photo on Horace's new camera. 'Smile, everyone!'

I think it sums up our Totally Amazing Summer:

The End (for now)

Love from
Harriet x

↖ and Tiger

HORACE'S DICTIONARY

Sometimes I have no idea what Horace is talking about, so I thought we should include these explanations of some of his funny expressions. Horace agreed and said, 'I have provided some assistance, in case any of you young whippersnappers have any trouble with my words!'

AMBUSCADE an attack or an ambush.

BARBARIAN a savage and uncivilized individual. Such as those pesky pigeons who foul my pillar!

BEHOLD to see or observe, especially something or someone impressive. For example, I imagine people often say: *Behold the mighty Horace*!

COMPATRIOT a fellow citizen. Harriet's fine grandfather is a compatriot.

DASTARDLY wicked or cruel. Angela's behaviour can be a touch dastardly.

DEIGN to give or grant something beneath oneself. For example: *I deigned to take Tiger for a walk.*

(DRIVELLING) DALCOP an insult. A dalcop is a silly person. If I am particularly vexed I like to add 'drivelling' in front of it, which means talking nonsense.

FINESSE I use this to mean delicate, refined and skilful.

FORSOOTH indeed, in truth.

FORTHWITH immediately!

FORTUITOUS something good that happens with a stroke of luck. It is most fortuitous that young Harriet befriended me in Princes Park.

FRATERNIZE to associate, talk to, or spend time with someone. Often used when the 'someone' is an unsuitable character, such as an enemy or a Silverbottom.

HARK listen!

HENCEFORTH from this moment in time. For example: *Henceforth, I shall always agree Horace is correct.*

INTELLIGENCE often used to mean cleverness or understanding, but it can also mean secret information.

LEAD CORRESPONDENT the head writer or journalist. I was head writer for *The Buzz* (for a time).

MORROW the following day. You might use 'tomorrow' but I prefer 'morrow'.

NAVAL something related to the navy or seagoing.

NAY no!

PERCHANCE perhaps. For example: *My pillar, perchance, is much better than the Silverbottom Mansion.*

POST-HASTE with the greatest speed.

POSTING an assignment to a job.

RESOLVED determined to do something, for example: I am resolved that everybody should wear a ruff.

SHENANIGANS mischievous behaviour. Some may say that mine and Barry's behaviour at the Stars of Stokendale awards was full of shenanigans.

SPLENDIFEROUS brilliant. Better than brilliant!

TOMFOOLERY silly nonsense.

UNCOMMON this can mean unusual or rare, but I tend to mean exceptional or remarkable.

VEXED very annoyed.

WHEREUPON after which. For example: *This morning I enjoyed a sandwich, whereupon I washed it down with some splendiferous pink lemonade!*

WHIPPERSNAPPER a young person who might not know everything.

ZARBLES an expression of surprise of my own creation.

LOVE HORACE AND HARRIET?
WHY NOT TRY THESE TOO!